To All the Penises I've Ever Known

Erotic Shorts
by
Lori Schafer

ISBN: 1942170440
ISBN-13: 978-1-942170-44-0

First Edition

DEDICATION

To RV, who motivated me to write my very first
piece of erotic flash fiction,
and
To Guy Hogan, for providing one of the earliest
markets for my work.

CONTENTS

ACKNOWLEDGMENTS

"Morning After" originally appeared in *Erotic Review Magazine* on July 7, 2014.

"Ballroom Dance" originally appeared in *The Pittsburgh Flash Fiction Gazette* on October 4, 2013.

"To All the Penises I've Ever Known" originally appeared in *The Pittsburgh Flash Fiction Gazette* on May 3, 2013.

"Me and Fat Marge" originally appeared in *Erotic Review Magazine* on July 7, 2013.

"Missed Connection" originally appeared in *The Pittsburgh Flash Fiction Gazette* on March 6, 2014.

"Lori Schafer: I Write Erotica" originally appeared in *The Pittsburgh Flash Fiction Gazette* on March 7, 2014.

MORNING AFTER

I yawned and pried open my eyes. Early morning sunlight was streaming in through the blinds. A cool breeze ruffled pleasantly through my exposed pubic hair. It tickled. I felt myself becoming aroused.

Wait a minute, I thought sleepily. A what was ruffling through my what now?

I glanced down at my body, dappled with the warming rays of the sun. My breasts were bare. My belly was bare. My thighs were bare. In fact, the only part of me that wasn't bare was my right foot, which still clung to the more stubborn half of a cotton ankle sock.

I closed my eyes and went back to sleep.

I was woken again by a soft cough somewhere off to my right. I kept my eyes shut and tried to ignore it. It sounded again, louder. I sighed and turned my head to look.

I'll admit I wasn't quite sure who I was going to find there. It isn't every day, you know, that a woman finds herself in this particular situation.

"Good morning, Kathy," Jim said, rising into a half-sitting position and smiling shyly at me, his dark eyes glowing.

"Er… good morning," I answered. I tried to smile back, but my face felt frozen. I didn't want to look at his eyes, so I looked at his body instead. Sure enough, he was naked, too. His penis had also risen into a half-sitting position, and it swayed gently as the cool breeze ruffled through his pubic hairs. Vaguely I wondered if it aroused him the way it did me.

"I guess this is a little weird, huh?" he said. He stretched a long hand out towards my hip, but stopped short of touching me.

"Oh," I said, not really sure what to say. "We've been friends a long time, Jim. I guess it was bound to happen eventually."

He inched closer. I wasn't sure if I was supposed to notice, so I pretended not to.

"Are we… okay?" he said, his eyes full of questions I didn't want to answer.

I took mental stock of my body, lying stark naked in a strange bed with sun trickling through the blinds. My breasts were sore. My thighs were sore. I felt like I'd been ridden hard and put away wet. All in all, it wasn't a bad way to wake up.

I turned back to him. He still had that arm hopefully extended and I took it and drew it around me. He pulled me toward him until my face was buried in his chest. He was covered with the smell of sweat and sex. He'd never smelled like that to me before. I didn't think I minded it.

"We're okay," I replied.

With a great heave of his long arms, he yanked me up on top of him and enveloped me in a big bear hug, his hands tight to my waist, his chest tight to my breast. Maybe if I'd had some warning, I could have resisted. But as it was, I couldn't help myself. I threw my legs around him. I felt his cock hardening and my insides responding. Wetness was already invading my thighs and I wondered where it had been hiding. This can't be a good idea, I thought. But that damned breeze was still ruffling irresistibly through my pubes and I didn't know what to do. If we did it again now, who knew where it might lead?

I shifted and his penis slid smoothly over my clit. It felt good, so I did it again. And again. He placed his hands on my ass and squeezed, hard. That made it even better. Maybe this wasn't such a bad idea after all.

"Starting without me, eh?" said a voice on my left.

"Morning, Sam," Jim said, not lessening his grip

on my ass.

"Morning, Sam," I echoed, still sliding that cock back and forth between my legs. "Sorry, didn't mean to wake you."

"Quite all right," he said, smiling at me with eyes that shined.

I paused to look him over. He, too, was completely naked, except for the pair of ladies silk panties strewn across his neck. I couldn't tell if the window-breeze was ruffling his pubes or not. There was too much fully erect cock in the way.

"This is a little weird, huh?" he said, his eyes fixed on me and Jim. He suddenly rolled toward us, sending the panties flying. He, too, smelled of sweat and sex. I thought maybe I liked it.

I shrugged. "We've been friends a long time, Sam," I said evenly. "It was bound to happen eventually."

He nodded his agreement. I nodded, too. Jim nodded back.

It's so wonderful when good friends agree.

Sam reached out to caress me with the back of his hand. My hips stopped moving. They were getting better ideas.

"Um, so what do we do now?" he said.

I didn't answer. Instead I rolled off of Jim and lay down between them. They cuddled up on each side of me, warming my body better than any early morning sunshine, their erections pressed hard against my thighs. Then they reached around me. I felt their fingers tickling my pubes and I forgot all about the breeze.

I spread my legs apart, as wide as they would go. There wasn't much room with them nestled beside me. The combined smell of sweat and sex was overpowering. Some of it was coming from me. I was sure now that I liked it.

"I don't know about you," I said. "But I'd like to be ridden hard and put away wet."

They snuggled in closer, reached underneath me, got their hands on my ass, and squeezed. I shifted and they both began stroking my clit. It was way better than when I did it.

"And what about tomorrow?" Jim asked me, his hands still busy below.

"Yeah, will we all still be friends?" Sam said, stroking me harder.

"No!" I gasped. "We – "

I couldn't finish my answer. My body was jerking in climax.

They waited while I was catching my breath. They lay with their heads on my breasts, their eyes searching mine. I looked out the window behind them. The sky was bright with sunshine. And so, I thought, was I.

I took their heads in my hands. Ran my fingers through their hair. Breathed in the smell of our sweat and sex. And kicked off the last half of that stubborn ankle sock. That was no good for riding.

"No," I said again, more gently this time. "We'll be something much better."

And I smiled.

The inspiration from this story came from my second novel, *Just the Three of Us: An Erotic Romantic Comedy for the Commitment-Challenged*. The style of this piece differs somewhat from that of my novel – the humor here is more restrained – but it's very much in the same vein. Frankly, I was delighted to revisit the concept because I really, really enjoyed writing that book. I love the characters, I love the setup, I even love the somewhat silly premise that three friends could just "happen" to fall in love in almost exactly the way that two friends might. In fact, I liked it so much that I'm halfway through writing the sequel. Plus I wrote this story. And then I got the idea for another short story called "Avalanche!" in which three friends… well, you get the drift.

The funny thing is, I never would have thought I'd find the whole threesome concept so intriguing. And honestly, I'm not sure that I really do. For me it's not threesomes in general, but more this particular threesome that's so endlessly amusing. Of course, maybe that's how it starts. Maybe it always begins with plain old monogamous, monamorous folks who, by chance, meet the two other people who make the perfect corners on that kind of triangle. One day you're hanging out with your best friends – the next you're in love. It could happen to you!

Okay, probably not. But don't discount the idea entirely, because you never know. And if it does happen, and it does work out, would you let me know? I could use another idea for a sequel...

BALLROOM DANCE

Tonight's the night. The grand finale, if you will. The final class in ballroom dance. The culmination of weeks of practice and training; the months of tedium through which I have suffered in order to arrive here, at the end, the final evening. The evening in which I may at last don my gown.

It's a beautiful gown, this pretty, antiquated garment. Cut low, bracingly low, low enough that even a deep breath may send my bulging breasts quivering into my admirers' anxiously waiting palms. Wearing it I will pity the modern woman who has cast aside such travesties of dress, not knowing, not recognizing the wondrous possibilities of the giant hoop skirt that, like a curtain, will conceal my naked undersides, the deep, dark crevices growing damp and moist with the heat of my body, the flush of my skin.

Yet they will pity me in my grandiose garb; will say to each other, "Oh, see how quickly she tires!" and perhaps they will be surprised when I retreat by myself to a sad, lonely corner while the others persist in the dance. Standing there all alone I will think of Henry, that husky-voiced fellow with the large hands I have so duly admired each time I've found myself swooning within them. He is also mysteriously missing from the dance floor, much as I am so strangely absent, here at the last. No one will dream where he has really gone. No one will even think it odd the way I will have my hands folded in front of me while I stand quietly in the corner, watching the action on the dance floor; the way my lips will part as if I am breathing rather heavily for a person who is not dancing.

And as the music continues no one will think it strange that more and more of the men retreat to the corner where I am so dejectedly standing, all worn out with dancing. Men tire, too, after all. What could be more natural than to see them gather in a circle at the far end of the room, chatting amongst themselves while the women continue to dance? No one will notice, against this masculine backdrop, when I turn slowly away towards the wall and rustle my skirts until Henry comes falling out, panting with the heat and exertion. No one will see me drop to my knees behind the concealing wall of men and unbuckle his belt and help myself to the refreshments within while my breasts protrude from their tidily-arranged cage, while he handles them with hard, groping fists as the others look on. No one will think it odd that one of the other men will help me to my feet; will, with the gentlest of rustles, again lift my skirt that another of his fellows might vanish beneath it.

And should the music threaten to draw to a close before I have taken and given as much I'd like of the other ballroom dancers, perhaps I shall widen my stance, lift my skirts higher, and invite two at a time to dive hungrily between my legs and sample the sweet juices within. And if they should fight; battle for prime position, perhaps I will enjoy that, too, the faces prowling, probing my nethers, the tongues licking and sticking and kissing where I most wish to be licked and sticked and kissed. Perhaps it will even be too much, two prodding, probing tongues for one hapless organ; perhaps I shall have to send one on another journey, around the other way while I hold their heads in my hands, one before me and the other behind.

And perhaps I will be so caught up in this music, my own music, the music of my body and theirs commingled into one, that I will fail to notice when the band stops playing, when the good men and women of this quaint suburban town abandon their positions and march towards the corner that I have so indelicately occupied in concert with the men who, like me, in the end, were more interested in pussy than dancing. Perhaps they will gather around, too, in horror and shock as I lift up my skirts to reveal one of their fellow-citizens nose-deep in my pussy, and an equally fine gentleman tongue-deep in my ass. Perhaps they will stand all around and watch while I scream and explode, while I spread my legs wide and plead piteously for more. Perhaps even as I drop to my knees to inhale the final cocks, to imbibe the last freshly squeezed juices of my partners in dance, some one of those fine citizens will feel it, too, the itch that I've got, and will come crawling forward on hands and knees to slide his own face underneath my still-hungry pussy, while I cover him discreetly over with the giant hoop skirt so that no one will see the shamelessness, the helplessness of my lust and his; of our lust and theirs.

I am ready; it is time. On to the dance.

Probably the less said about this piece, the better! Although I had already been writing and publishing erotic work for some months when this story first came out, there was something about this particular piece that was so over the top of the naughty sex scale that I didn't even want to promote it. What if my boss read it?!

It certainly does possess a depth of dirtiness that

goes beyond that of most of my sexually explicit work. But I suspect I have more of this type of piece lurking somewhere inside me. At some point, when I feel like taking a break from writing novels, I thought it might be fun to put together a series of short stories like this. I've even got a title picked out: *I've Got an Itch*.

Just don't tell my boss.

TO ALL THE PENISES
I'VE EVER KNOWN

Yours, little brother of my best friend, was the first one I ever saw. We were five and you were four. One summer afternoon when there were no grownups around you dropped your shorts to take a leak on a bush in our backyard. Your penis dangled limply, almost absurdly in its shriveled laxity, and seemed to me no more noteworthy than my own peeing-mechanism. But that night I dreamt that we found a garden snake in the yard, a snake that blew up like a monstrous red balloon and devoured us all. Freud would have been proud.

You, stepfather, revealed yours to me without ever knowing it. I was self-sufficient at the age of eight, and an early riser, and one Sunday morning while I was eating my cereal and reading the funnies in the kitchen you emerged from the bedroom you shared with my mom to fetch the rest of the newspaper from the doorstep of our apartment. Did you have to do that entirely naked? I did not need to see you that way, my newest dad, did not need forever after to be stuck with the image of that penis, so much longer than my best friend's little brother's, wider, thicker, and half-erect. But any chance that I might have forgotten it vanished when I glimpsed it again not long after, through the ventilation grating by the floor in the wall between my bedroom and the bathroom. I wasn't peeking, honest; I heard funny noises coming from the bathroom and wondered whether I should be scared of whatever was in there, but it was just you on the toilet, pooping, that penis hanging down again between your legs, pointing right at me where I was squatting on the other side of the wall.

Your penis, my puppy love, my high school sweetheart, was the first I ever touched, ever held, ever took into my mouth and body. It was yours that I squeezed too hard or not hard enough, yours that I learned to protect and to be protected from, yours that was not only a penis but part of a package that conformed so neatly to the cupping of my hand. Your body was still growing then, and your penis was, too: the sweetly modest member of the boy I had loved transformed into the stern soldier of the man I didn't.

Yours, my cocky, confident friend with benefits,

was oversized overall, but I wasn't aware of that then; I knew only that I never seemed to have enough room to contain it all. Yours was the one I measured, so I might in future have a basis for comparison, and although you didn't object, I think I embarrassed you with my giggles and my ruler. I wondered afterwards if you ever knew how you stacked up against other men, and if you did, whether that was what gave you your self-assurance.

You, my college chums, casual boyfriends, victims of my capricious lust, introduced me to a variety of penises, short and long, thick and thin, curved and straight. You had brown ones and red ones and black ones and purple ones – though I never liked to look at the purple ones much. You gave them to me in many forms and guises, from different directions, and at different angles, and different speeds. And you let me pat them fondly and be on my way without lingering, without embracing, without promising if or when I would see you or them again.

Your penises, you miscellaneous, meaningless men I met after college but didn't especially care for, yours were as immemorable as your faces, your bodies, your spirits. Not one of yours could I pick out of a lineup, not one do I recollect fondly, not one among them did I ever really want to have or to own, but every now and again I still needed to have, even if I did not need to own.

But then came yours, my love, my life, my happily-ever-after, the penis to put an end to all the other penises. For sometimes it is red, and sometimes brown, and when you hold me one way it is large, and in another small; you curve it into me when it needs to be curved, and straighten it when it should be straight, and if I want it to be fast, it is fast, and when I want slow, it is slow. From you I learned that it is not the penis that matters, but the man who stands behind it. Truth be told, I don't even look at your penis much anymore; mostly only when you're climbing out of the shower and it's dangling there all shrunken and lifeless and resembling very much in form, if not in size, the first penis I ever saw. Your penis may be different from all of the others, but it is also exactly the same. And that is how I know that there is more to being a man than having a penis, because after all these years, and all those penises, I've kept coming back only to yours.

This "open letter" was one of the first short pieces I wrote after deciding to become a writer. Of course, once I'd written it, I had no idea what to do with it. Clearly it wasn't a story for the literary journals – although I did try a few. It was too graphic for most online magazines, and not graphic enough for "adult" sites. Then I happened to stumble across

The Pittsburgh Flash Fiction Gazette online. Featured on its front page were a flash fiction story and a handful of naked ladies. That, I knew then, was the right market for this piece.

Sexuality can be a difficult subject to tackle, and it's something I've struggled a lot with in my books. Not because I'm uncomfortable writing about it, but because sex in literature is often relegated to the realms of pornography or erotica, and my work, while often sexually explicit, rarely falls neatly into either of those categories. But sex in writing does not have to be all about titillation. It doesn't have to be all about arousal and consummation, nor about the quest for some idealized partner and the ever-elusive simultaneous orgasm. It doesn't even have to be dramatic. It can be stupid. It can be funny. Why not? Sex makes us stupid and funny. There are many ways of exploring sexuality, that endlessly fascinating aspect of our lives as human beings. "To All the Penises I've Ever Known" was one of mine.

ME AND FAT MARGE

I look with pity at my old friend Brent, his warm brown eyes so filled with sadness that tears are threatening to trickle down his usually buoyant cheeks. It's the first time I've visited Middle-of-Nowheresville since my friend's wedding nearly a year before, and my heart aches to find him so disconsolate.

"Where's Marge?" I say, looking around for his new bride, a pretty, plump, charmer of a woman with a sparkling personality and a passion for creative cookery.

He swallows. "In there," he says, shrugging a shoulder towards the slider opening onto the living room.

I look at the enormous woman sprawled sideways upon a full-sized bed, staring mournfully at an empty tray as if willing it to refill itself. She's

18

draped only in a loose sheet and I'm not surprised; it must be both difficult and expensive to find clothes for a woman so large. Her breasts alone are the size of honeydews and as I stare, my eyes popping, at the nipples poking through the thin cotton I wonder, in spite of myself, if they're equally as sweet.

"That can't be healthy," I observe, yanking my mind forcibly out of the gutter and attempting to calm the sudden, unexpected itch now tickling my own modest breasts.

He nods glumly. "Her doctor's worried about her heart and I am, too. The psychologist says it's an oral fixation or something. She barely even talks now, but she can't stop eating. I don't even take her out anymore; the neighbors can't afford to feed her."

She's staring hungrily about, and I can't help but think that I know what I'd be chowing down on if I had enormous tits like those, gigantic enough to reach with my tongue. The itch starts in again but I force it down so I can ponder my friend's problem instead.

Within seconds I've got an idea. I guess it doesn't take long when your mind's always moving in the same direction. I'm not quite sure how to say it, so I straighten my hair and glasses, tuck my hand up under my chin as if I'm deep in thought, and then give it to him with all of the scientific seriousness I can muster.

"Has she sucked your dick lately, Brent?" I inquire politely.

"What?!" he yelps back.

"Your penis," I clarify, thinking that maybe "dick" is a colloquialism unknown in this decidedly rural part of the country. "Have you been giving it to her to suck on?"

"Well, uh…" he says, his cheeks reddening as if suddenly flushed with fever. "Under the circumstances, no, not lately."

"I was just thinking… seems like that would suit her oral fixation, doesn't it?" I prod.

"I guess you're right!" he exclaims suddenly, beaming. "Marge! Oh, Marge!"

He throws open the sliding door to the parlor and I follow, waving to Marge from the doorway. "Good to see you, Kat!" she calls, the expulsion of air causing those tantalizing breasts to sway like an inviting backyard hammock caught in a soothing summer breeze.

I watch as Brent settles his hips in front of her face and thrusts his dick ardently into her hungry, open mouth. She swallows it as eagerly as a vacuum cleaner on shag-pile carpeting and he groans in response. I try hard not to be jealous, but they're both making a lot of wet mm-mmm noises and pretty soon I'm wondering if the mailman will be coming by soon or if I should order a pizza and hope for a nubile delivery boy.

Just as I'm starting to think I'm going to have to call on a neighbor or, even worse, take care of things myself, Brent lets out a loud "Yahhhhh!" and forces his cock up to the balls down his wife's wide-open throat, whereupon she swallows noisily and then lets out a satisfied, gurgling sigh. He pulls away, drizzling little droplets down Marge's fine, full breasts, and do you know what she says next, this brilliant, adorable woman after my own heart?

"More!"

"Thanks, honey," Brent says placatingly. "But you know I can't do that again so soon, right?" He lays a hand on his wiener and flops it helplessly towards her, its magnificent purple splendor reduced now to the color and consistency of a very fat earthworm. It's not the most appealing sight, but Marge keeps staring at it like it's the gourmet concoction she's been yearning for all along.

"More!" she insists.

Brent turns to me, at a loss as to what to do. I get another idea. I'm not entirely certain he's going to like it, and I swallow nervously. But, being the good friend that I am, I'm willing to sacrifice myself in the interest of his wedded bliss.

"Um, well, if she just needs something to do with her mouth…" I begin, maneuvering my knees apart and hoping he'll get the picture.

He doesn't. He stares at me blankly until finally

I point with two fingers at the space between my legs and say, "You know, she could put her lips on my, you know..." Drool floods my cheeks and I swallow again.

"Oh!" he replies, his neck flushing crimson like he's had a sudden attack of the heebie-jeebies and isn't sure yet whether he likes it. A bit of spittle starts to leak out of the corner of his mouth and before he can even say, "I guess that would be all right," I've ripped off my skirt and pantyhose and am sitting backwards straddling that wide open mouth.

Now, I have had pussy-lickings before. Many pussy-lickings, in fact; more than I can even count, although for some strange reason I still never seem to get my fill. But I'll tell you this, there is no one who knows how to lick a pussy like a person who has spent a lot of time exercising their mouth. She doesn't just eat that pussy; she devours it. And before I know it, I'm left panting in a wilted heap on her gigantic breasts and taking mouthfuls of them like they're chocolate-dipped ice cream cones while she's up there behind my ass saying "More!"

What choice do I have? I give her my comparatively tiny breasts to suckle until they're all wet and worn and then help her get a handful of her own masses up to her mouth so she can nibble greedily on those for a while. That, of course, gets Brent going again, so he gives her another, much longer round of cock in the face and that last bit of juice seems to satisfy her because she finally drops off to sleep, her face a mask of blissful contentment.

"I really think this could work," Brent whispers, gleefully observing Marge's tranquil dream state. "She hasn't even asked for food since we started."

"How long do you think we can keep this up?" I wonder, my mind reeling delightedly out of control at the thought of weeks, perhaps months of oral pleasure on the face of a master. In my mind I've already taken a leave of absence and made plans to relocate to Middle-of-Nowheresville for as long as it takes. Then I remember that big contract I'm supposed to be landing and my dirty dreams disperse like hot fumes from a steam engine, leaving me wilted. "I mean, she can lick my pussy all day as far as I'm concerned, but I'm supposed to be leaving town tomorrow."

His face sets into a tough, hardened expression. "I'll find a way," he says with determination. "I would do anything to ensure my wife's happiness. Anything."

I don't know what he means by that, but, assuming it involves drastic measures he doesn't want to confide, I don't press him further.

Well, after a little while Marge wakes up and I can hardly wait to get on board that amazing mouth again, especially when I know my time with this marvel of the natural world is doomed to be so short. So short, but oh, so sweet. I straddle my hips across her nose and she dives into me like I'm as smooth as a chocolate crème pie and twice as tasty and I do what I can to gorge her with my own creaminess before Brent can give her some more of his. Then I burrow my head between her monstrous melons while he goes at her face again, thrusting over and over for minutes on end, but she never seems to get tired of sucking, as I note with admiration. And when he finally blows his top, she shoves him gruffly out of the way and taps me on the shoulder and I realize with boundless joy that it's my turn to hop on again. Who says insatiable is a bad thing?

We keep it up like that all through the long night, and my legs are wobbling like canned jelly when I finally haul my soggy ass out to my car to go to the train station. Marge is still sleeping peacefully. I can swear she looks thinner already.

"Good luck, Brent," I say as I'm leaving. "Try to keep her on track; it's for her own good."

"I know it is," he answers. "Don't worry, I've got a plan."

He gives me a funny little salute and I drive away, already longing again for Marge's magnificent face on my worshipping pussy.

It's a full three months before business again brings me back to town, and I hurry over to Brent and Marge's as soon as I can, hoping against hope that she's gotten herself healthy. Not getting an answer when I ring the bell, I try the knob and it jiggles open. Cautiously I peer inside. The living-room bed on which Marge once lay is gone, and for a moment I fear the worst. Then I hear slurping noises and, taking a step inside, see a stout and entirely naked young woman hard at work on her knees inhaling the very large cock of a very large postman who's very loudly expressing his enjoyment of it. Thinking that Brent and Marge must have moved while I was away, I turn to make a quiet exit and bump my head with an audible thunk against the lintel.

"Ow!" I exclaim, causing the couple to turn to me and stare.

"Hello!" the strange woman cries in welcome, as if I were an expected visitor. "Hold on just a minute, will you?"

She goes back to the cock and I'm getting itchy listening to all that slurping but fortunately he finishes up pretty quickly and then casually buckles up his trousers as if he does this every day.

"See you tomorrow!" he calls out cheerfully as he heads out the door.

"Thanks again!" she yells back through the open doorway, in which she is standing as if entirely unabashed about being naked on the doorstep. My kind of woman, I think.

I think it more when she slides her way back over towards me and, dropping heavily to her knees as if kneeling was her favorite position, says sultrily, "I've been wanting another taste of this for a long time." Then she proceeds to yank down my skirt and panties and plunge headfirst into my pussy like it's a hot fudge sundae doppled all over with the thickest whipped cream and decorated with the sweetest, tangiest maraschino cherries you've ever imagined tasting.

"Marge!" I exclaim, pitching headlong toward orgasm before she's even brought out her fancy moves. "I can't believe it's you!" I pant, my body jerking in spasms of uncontrolled ecstasy as she trains her tongue around each of my most intimate curves.

"Oh, yes," she explains, burying my face in her bountiful breasts as she clutches me to her in a warm, friendly hug. "Your plan worked great. I've already lost almost a hundred pounds and Brent and I have never been happier. Oh, there he is now!" she cries, dusting off her kneecaps and running to the door, her now only cantaloupe-sized breasts bouncing provocatively with each flouncing step.

"Hi, honey, I'm home!" he yells as if he can't see her standing naked before him, her head already bobbing towards his still-packaged cock.

"Isn't she great?" he says to me as she pops his penis wholeheartedly into her eager mouth. "It's all thanks to you, you know."

"But how… how do you…?" I ask, thinking of the mailman who's so recently departed.

"Oh, she keeps busy. Around town, you know. Maybe some husbands wouldn't be able to handle that but, you know what? I love my wife, and I want her to be happy and healthy."

He pauses to let out a pleasured groan while Marge's enthusiasm continues unabated. "And you know what else? We're the most popular couple in town now. Seems everyone wants to have us over. Marge is so outgoing, you know."

Watching her bob her head on his cock, making those mm-mmm noises like it's a fresh cherry pie, I can't help but agree.

"Well, I'm back now, too, for a while," I remind him. "So if you need any help with her, I'm happy to do it," I volunteer bravely.

"That's real sweet," he says appreciatively. "But you don't have to do that again. We've found plenty of people who are happy to help her out, and I know you're not really into that; you were just being the really good friend that you are. Oh, wait, hold on a sec."

He plunges his cock hard into her face and she swallows it as if she was born into the circus and then emerges, her face shining, her mouth open, little bits of jizz and what I think is my pussy juice drying in tantalizing bits about her lips. She sticks her tongue out at me and my thighs grow wet in response, and all of a sudden I really miss big fat Marge.

Ah, my first published foray into true erotica! It was a big step and one that, frankly, for a long time I wasn't sure I was ready to make. I don't want to see myself getting pigeon-holed into only one kind of writing and erotica, ironically enough, can be a turnoff for some people. Besides, there's an internal cringing factor to erotic writing that I don't think you get with sci-fi or historical fiction or other genres. For example, while I was writing my first novel, *My Life with Michael*, I frequently found myself becoming embarrassed in composing the raunchier scenes. I mean, embarrassed sitting all by myself in front of my computer, without anyone even reading it. And those were fairly standard sex scenes - nothing particularly kinky. But like anything else, I guess you get used to it after a while. My second book, *Just the Three of Us*, being a threesome story, is about a hundred times dirtier – what, in the Romance industry, they would term a Heat Level of 4+ – and that didn't even faze me.

Anyway, in between novel chapters I took to dabbling in some short-story erotica, and "Me and Fat Marge" was one of the first products of that effort. What I like most about it is the fact that it's funny, which I think is somewhat of a rarity in the genre. Odd, isn't it? Sex and humor seem as if they ought to go together hand in... well, you assemble the metaphor!

MISSED CONNECTION

"Christopher," I breathed, almost silently, internally, my suitcase falling unhindered from my faltering hand as he approached, staring quizzically towards me in dumb disbelief; or worse, I feared, in dumbfounded dismay. What was he doing here?

Involuntarily I flushed, color screaming into my cheeks at the recollection of the unbelievably foolish thing I had done, that dreadfully stupid day nearly a year before when I'd learned that he was moving, never to return to this city I still called home. That letter I'd hand-delivered to his office, not even asking to see him, not really wanting to; knowing that once he'd read it I never could see him again, never would want to; would be confined to thinking of him only in the guise of the fantasies I'd so recklessly confided into the eternal silence of his imminent absence. Written depictions of imaginary scenes so graphic that my hair kinked and grayed merely to think of them; deeply personal secrets of my inner life that never before had I dared to share; that never before had I conceived with such indomitable passion.

It was inscrutable, this flatly expressionless face now pushing across the airport lobby towards me and instinctively I backed away; retreated stumbling backwards until I pressed up against the wall beyond the boarding area and could flee no further. Yet still he came, perhaps horrified, perhaps disgusted and offended by what I had done, and I could only watch helplessly, pinned against the cool blue tile, as he neared to within twenty feet, ten, five, two.

He stared, confronting me with his impenetrable thoughts, assailing me with his forbidding silence while I stared back, still scared, still shocked into speechlessness. And then abruptly he dropped his luggage and closed the gap between us from two feet to two inches and pressed me hard, harder up against the airport wall, his thick, sturdy arms encircling my waist, his chest crushing against mine in a powerful embrace. And suddenly his eyes were no longer incomprehensible, but warm and kind, and they gazed into mine without hesitation, without a trace of uncertainty. Roughly he pulled my torso towards him, away from the wall growing hot against my backside, his hands penetrating the thin fabric of my dress as they travelled down my back, over my hips, and around my buttocks, squeezing my cheeks tightly, tantalizingly in fierce, fervent fists. Grasping my naked thighs, he spread them, wide, then wider, and dizzily I relished the sensation of the air rushing through the space between them as he gathered my legs about his waist, pushed my back up against the wall, and tickled his thumbs over the firm, sensitive muscles of my unguarded groin.

He nuzzled between my open legs and without stopping to think, I pulled him eagerly forward, the blunted cloth of his khakis growing damp with my wetness as I stroked myself against him, feeling his cock so close, so unbearably close that I couldn't believe that it wasn't inside me, that it was still relegated to the realm of teasing anticipation. With heavy hands he clasped at my breasts and they swelled; met his fingers with equally greedy anticipation while he shoved his pelvis against mine, thrust it urgently towards me, almost into me, causing the skirt of my dress to fall away, laying my legs bare and my ass barer, only the silk of my thong standing between me and my pussy and the object of our mutual desire.

"Last call for Flight 751," a booming voice interrupted and reluctantly Christopher drew away, gently lowering my aching body back to the floor in a sad, lonely descent from the height of passion into the depths of despair.

He gazed at me again with his kind, caring eyes and for the briefest of moments pressed his lips against mine; a sparse, unsatisfactory kiss that left my tongue hungering for more, for even the slightest bit more. But already he had lifted his suitcase; was glancing forlornly towards the gate that even now was threatening to close.

"Where were you all week?" he said wistfully as he strode hurriedly away; not waiting for an answer; knowing, like I did, that it was too late to matter. I stood and watched as he vanished down the passageway, back towards his new faraway home. And then retrieved my own suitcase from where I'd dropped it, and took a taxi to my own.

It had been nothing like my fantasies, I thought that evening as I inscribed a new letter to Christopher, one that he might, someday, still want to read; one that I someday might even send. In my dreams the deed was never half-done. In my dreams he was only half-gone.

This piece is particularly interesting because I actually wrote two versions of it. "Delayed Connection," which I've included in my *Romance Shorts* collection, is sweet, romantic, and non-explicit. "Missed Connection," which was the first version of the story built around this scenario, is a much more sexual and also strangely sadder piece. However, the initial premise for both pieces was actually not, as you might think, the chance meeting at the airport. Rather it was about the confession with which the story begins. Because I think we can all relate to that, to the regrets we have over the "one that got away," over never making a move when we had the chance. How afraid we were to share our feelings, for fear of being rejected, yet how simultaneously eager we were to admit them, on the unlikely chance that our emotional and/or physical affection would be returned. The narrator here has taken the bold and incredibly foolish step of actually making the confession – in writing, no less – not in the middle of the acquaintance, but after it's too late for anything to happen between her and her object of desire.

What could possibly motivate a character to do something like that? There's nothing in it for her, obviously, nothing to be gained but an increase in her pain and humiliation, so why would she do it? The answer is simply that she wanted him to know. At the very last, she wanted him to know how attractive he was to her, and what kind of fantasies he inspired, even if it meant exposing her deepest secrets to someone who had already left her behind. It's a remarkably unselfish act. Stupid, surely, but unselfish.

I'd like to say that she's rewarded for making

this unusual parting gift, and perhaps, in a way, she is. In the end, she still doesn't get what she wants. But maybe she feels a bit better about not getting it. And if you find yourself grieving over a long-lost love, you would be foolish to hope for more than that.

COMPLETE YOUR ASSIGNMENTS!

She stared at it, the short brown oar hanging conspicuously on the wall behind her new Professor's desk, mounted on hooks beneath a stenciled wooden sign that threatened "Complete your assignments!"

"I see Ms. Johnson has discovered the classroom's discipline stick," Professor Clark chuckled, recapturing her attention.

"Discipline stick, sir?" she said, fixing her gaze upon him.

He laughed. An attractive man in his late thirties, he didn't fit the stereotype of the stuffy college professor.

"Yes," he said, bringing it over for her to examine. "This college was constructed in the eighteenth century. The founders believed in the strict enforcement of school discipline – and the application of corporal punishment as the most effective means of achieving it. They wrote into the bylaws that students who failed to submit their assignments be 'paddled upon their bare bottoms, with a minimum of ten strokes, in front of the class, that their punishment might serve as a warning to other potential offenders.' "

There was tittering all around the classroom.

"Technically the rule still exists," he said, pointing a threatening finger at her. "So let that be a warning to you, Ms. Johnson!"

She ran her fingers over it, this paddle that had doled out countless strokes of its painful and humiliating punishment. It, too, was not what she had expected. The wood was smooth, almost polished even, and it slipped beneath her fingers without a hint of a sliver or a scratch. She imagined how it would look in a man's rough, strong fist, how he might wield it hard, like a weapon, or gentle, like a hand.

"Bend over, Miss," he'd say, lifting it down from the wall.

She'd stand uncertainly before him, glancing with embarrassment at the students staring all around her, their faces frozen in surprise and awe.

He would nod sternly. "Now, Miss. Facing the class."

She'd turn her back on the classroom and lean at an angle over his massive wooden desk. She'd feel her breasts falling forward, filling out the cleavage that no one but she would see. And her skirt lifting upward, threatening to expose her entire underneath.

He would approach, half-smiling, half-grim, cradling the paddle almost lovingly in his arms.

"Remove your underthings, Miss," he'd say, stroking the paddle's edge. Reluctantly she'd obey, sliding her fingers beneath her skirt and around to her hips. She'd pull them down slowly, oh, so very slowly, delaying the inevitable, wiggling them gently over the curves of her buttocks and thighs until they fell, freed, down to the floor.

"Lift your skirt," he'd direct her, and she would do it, drawing it up over her waist, feeling it fall against the small of her back while the other students gasped at the sight of her buttocks, now completely exposed.

He'd step towards her and then press the paddle lightly against her bottom, testing it. She'd feel it sliding across her buttocks, soft from wear and warm from his hand. He'd push down on her backside and she'd bend over further, assuming the position he required. Then he'd push again and she'd spread her legs wider and know, from the chill that shivered beneath her, that more than her ass was now bared to the room.

Without warning he would smack her, hard with the paddle, and she'd cry out with pain and surprise, then tense herself to await the next blow. It would come, sending shivers across her buttocks and throughout her body, until again she would feel the hard sting of wood on her ass. She'd twist her neck around and catch a glimpse of the classroom, the young men watching her, fascinated, the young women, horrified. He'd strike her again and they would jump, their eyes fixed on her rump, and she would jump, too, crying out again, wondering how many blows he would give her, how long it would be before this humiliation was over.

"You may go back to your seat now," he'd say at last, raising her from his desk and folding her skirt back down over her bottom. "Although you may prefer to stand."

She'd stoop to retrieve her panties and then retire to a corner of the classroom and tentatively touch her bottom. It would still sting, and when she examined it, it would be red from where he'd struck her, over and over, glowing from the punishment she'd so sorely deserved.

"I trust no one has neglected to do the assignment?" Professor Clark said the following morning, smiling cheerfully around the room at his students. "I won't have to break out the paddle, will I, Ms. Johnson?"

He nodded towards the wall. She gazed again at the paddle, so strict, so menacing, so firm. And hurriedly closed her notebook, the one containing the formulas she'd spent half the night figuring.

She rose from her desk and strode to the front of the class. She heard the other students gasp as she leaned hard over the Professor's desk, and again as she removed her underwear. With a flick of her wrists she lifted her skirt and there she was, exposed, ready for punishment.

"I'm afraid you will, Professor," she said. "I didn't complete the assignment."

She smiled grimly as, visibly stunned, he reached to retrieve the paddle. She was going to fail this class, she thought as she felt her cheeks tingling with excitement. But it would be worth it!

Um…no comment!

WEEKEND AWAY

"I was thinking maybe we could go away for the weekend," Jesse said, interrupting my post-coital attempt at slumber. He hadn't quite gotten the hang of my no-talking-after-sex rule yet. It didn't really matter, though; I wasn't listening anyway.

"Um-hmm," I answered sleepily, touching the tip of my tongue to the roof of my mouth. It tasted like semen. Or maybe it was my tongue that tasted like semen; maybe my mouth just tasted like mouth.

"Really?" he said brightly. "You want to?" I half-tilted my head towards him and he bent down off his elbow to kiss me. His mouth tasted like pussy. His tongue did, too.

"Want to what?" I answered, rolling over onto the side on which I always slept, hoping that would prompt him to get going. I did think it was polite the way he always waited until I was asleep to leave.

41

Of course, he never had to wait very long.

"Go away for the weekend," he repeated.

I sat straight up, my breasts snapping to attention as they jerked to a halt in front of me. This was not the kind of big bang I'd been expecting when I'd asked him to come over tonight.

"You mean, like, a trip somewhere? I don't know, Jesse," I said with trepidation, staring hard at him as if he'd suggested something highly irregular. He had, after all. We were only supposed to be friends with benefits. A weekend away sounded suspiciously like a "couple" kind of deal.

"Come on, Cindy," he urged, scootching over to me and bundling me up in his arms like a hairy haystack. "Wouldn't you like to get sweaty someplace else for a change?" he prompted, purposefully pressing his loose limbs into all of my good places.

I looked at him and sighed. I never had been able to resist that man. Even when he didn't smell like fresh pussy.

"Where did you have in mind?" I asked, thinking I was bound to regret asking.

"Not far, not far," he answered hurriedly, scrambling to grab his pants up off the floor and digging a brochure out of the back pocket. "See, there's a lake here, only a couple of hours north of us. We can rent a cabin." He studied me hopefully.

"A couple of hours?" I said doubtfully. "Sounds

like a long drive."

"No longer than that trip we took to the city that time," he reminded me.

"Yeah, but that was before we – " I stopped short. I didn't know why it mattered. We'd always spent a lot of time together, even before the clothes started coming off. But I guess I thought it was safer, somehow, to minimize our non-naked activities now that we were engaging in so many naked ones. "Before we were all old and stiff and stuff," I corrected myself.

"You were thirty-nine!" he retorted.

"And now I'm forty," I replied. "What if my hip goes out?"

"Then I guess that'll mean no more nookie for you," he responded.

The horror must have shown in my face, because in seconds he was clutching me tightly to his chest and brushing his close-cropped beard apologetically against my chin.

"I'm so sorry, sweetheart," he said. "I didn't know what I was saying. I'm sure that will never happen to you!"

"What did you call me?" I answered suspiciously.

He ignored me. "Next weekend," he said, wagging a threatening finger at me. "Or there really will be no nookie for you!"

"All right, you've got me," I said. "Now could

you hush up so I can get some sleep?"

But I didn't sleep. I lay silently with my eyes convincingly closed until I heard him rise and dress and walk out into the night. I felt a little bad about that, as I always did. Seemed a bit cruel, really, to make a man get up and go home after sex. I know I wouldn't have done it. That was why I always insisted in meeting at my place. That, and so when I woke up smelling like Jesse, I could go and shower without offending him. Although I wasn't usually finicky about sex juices, he had this really amazing smell, and I found it distracting having it on me all the time. It was better to wash it off and be able to go on with my day.

The following weekend came, and we survived the trip all right. Except that Jesse kept going on and on about how much fun it was going to be, and how if it worked out well maybe we could go someplace else together before the summer was over. I mysteriously managed to find a multitude of my absolute favorite songs playing on the radio and had to crank it up full blast until he changed the subject.

By the time we arrived, though, neither of us was talking much. We were too parched. He wasn't kidding when he said we'd be getting sweaty. It was early August, and it was scorching when we checked into our cabin. I couldn't even tell you what the place was like because it was so frightfully hot that we barely glanced at it as we changed into our swimsuits and then hurried down towards the semi-private beach.

From our door, the lake appeared cool, restful, and inviting. As we drew nearer, it actually seemed to be steaming in the sun. I was sweating uncontrollably and was elated to be out of my clothes, but in minutes even my bathing suit was wet with a sticky combination of perspiration and sunscreen. I discretely lifted my arm and took a whiff. Rotten coconuts. Fortunately Jesse didn't seem to notice. He smelled as amazing as ever. The perspiration even seemed to enhance his aroma, like juice dripping from meat roasting on a spit. I tried to be discreet as I wiped away my drool. Jesse could be surprisingly sensitive on matters like that; I wasn't quite sure how he would take being compared to fresh meat.

We had left the shaded area and were baking like pizzas in the outdoor oven when Jesse finally said, "I can't take any more. Water?"

"Water!" I agreed. We both raced toward it and then into it, not slacking up as it climbed past our knees, waists, and chests. I tried to pretend that it didn't rankle me when he outpaced me. Not very successfully, I'm afraid.

"I win!" he cried.

"Pshaw!" I answered. "I totally let you win!"

"Oh, you did not!"

"Okay, maybe not," I conceded. "But I bet I can outswim you!"

And then proceeded to prove my point by lying back in the still water and stretching out into my elementary backstroke. I was a very good glider, and in six strokes I had pulled a pool's length away from him.

"Hey!" he yelled. "Where are you going?"

He sounded a little concerned, so I pulled up and began treading water, the way it should be done, not strenuously but real relaxed, languidly stroking with my hands and feet in turn. When he finally came abreast of me, panting heavily, I shot him a glance of superiority and pulled out my sidestroke and executed it in tight circles around him.

"See?" I gloated. "I can swim circles around you!"

He thwarted me through an unfair advantage – he remembered to use his brain instead of his body. When I came around for the next pass, he latched onto my bikini top, and before I knew it, he had jerked on the two strings that untied it, lifted it off my chest, and rendered me topless.

"Hey!" I shouted. "Give that back!"

"Not until you admit I'm a better swimmer than you!"

"Never!!" I yelled defiantly.

He took my top and strung it around his neck,

about which it hung limply, emptied of boobies. My breasts were floating comfortably, perkily, even, in the lake water, but I refused to let that arouse me in light of the competition we had going. Two can play at that game, I thought. Without warning I dove down fast and grabbed hold of his swimsuit and yanked it down to his ankles. He was kicking to beat the band but he needed his arms, too, to keep him afloat so he was nearly powerless to stop me. I was almost out of breath when I finally got them off, and with my final stroke, I kicked away from him in order to preserve my freedom of movement. He began paddling towards me as soon as I surfaced, but I frog-kicked away again while debating what to do with his trunks. They wouldn't have fit around my neck even if I'd wanted to store them there, and they wouldn't have stayed put on any other part of my body, so finally I knotted the drawstring to the right cord on my own string bikini, where it flapped eerily against my skin like seaweed or some unseen slimy water creature. Unfortunately, this required a lot of strenuous kicking and most of my attention, and I didn't notice that he was drawing nearer to me until he lunged suddenly at my hips and I felt my bottom coming loose and then, horror of horrors, vanishing from between my thighs.

I inhaled sharply and quickly reversed directions, gaping down into the water seeking my lost swimsuit. For a second I thought I spotted a flash of fuchsia and I grabbed for it, but nothing came up in my fingers and then it was gone.

"Gotcha!" he proclaimed triumphantly.

"Got yourself, too!" I sputtered. "Both of our bottoms are gone now!" I explained what had happened.

"Hmm," he said when I was done. "Well, it's only a five-minute walk back to the cabin, so that should be fine, right?"

I pulled my bikini top tight around his neck by the elastic and then let it go. Thwap!, it resounded as it whacked him on the face and neck. "Oof!" he exclaimed, when I snapped him again, harder.

Gratifying as that was, it didn't solve the problem. We were still mostly naked and had a long walk back. Well, long for naked people, anyway. We swam cautiously close to the shore. I waited for my feet to scrape bottom, and then scuttled along like a crab with my body underwater until I'd reached the shallowest place I could get to and still be covered. Jesse followed suit.

I held my breath as we surveyed the scene. I could see no one, not on the beach, not in the water, not among the trees. The landscape appeared devoid of humanity, and in a brief, nonsensical flash, I wondered if we were all that was left and it was up to us to repopulate the earth, which would be unfortunate because at our age I didn't think we would succeed. I tried to prick up my ears to listen, but then I remembered that my ears didn't do that so I cupped them with my hands instead, listening for laughter, voices, music, any sound that might signify people and not plants or animals. I heard nothing. It was eerily still. How could there be no one else here on such a hot weekend day? Jesse was straining his eyes and ears, too, but had apparently also detected nothing to fear, for after a little while he looked at me and nodded. I nodded back.

And then we were standing, rising up from the water, and as the droplets cascaded down my naked body I imagined myself as a mortal and less awe-inspiring version of Aphrodite, and Jesse as Poseidon, except with, um, only one prong in his trident. I couldn't recall my mythology well enough to know how closely related that made us, but under the circumstances I decided not to fret over it. The dripping continued as we waded slowly towards shore, trying not to make waves or gurgling noises as we picked our feet up from the muddy lake bottom and set them down again. The coast was still clear as we reached solid ground and, as if by unspoken mutual agreement, we strode quite naturally along, perhaps a little faster than we normally would have in our bare feet. There would be opportunities to slink behind trees and bushes if someone came. But until then we marched erect and proud, unhampered by shame or clothing. Jesse looked as handsome as he ever did in the buff, except for that stupid bikini top still dangling from his neck, which clashed horribly with the auburn shade of his hair.

Aha! I thought. We do still have one article of clothing! I reached for it, but he leaned away from my grasp.

"What?" I whispered. "It's mine, isn't it?"

"Sorry," he whispered back. "Wieners are hardcore. I need it more than you."

We had reached the small wooded area between the cabin and the beach. I'd cooled off in the lake, and now the sun was streaming through the trees and it felt pleasantly warm on my body as the water evaporated. There was still no sign of anyone nearby.

"Then why aren't you wearing it?" I muttered.

And with that, he pulled the top up over his head and began attempting to fashion it into some kind of cover for his penis. The first attempt resulted in more of a sling than a cover, and I giggled silently at the sight of his junk swinging along in a hammock as we walked. Next he tied one of the breast-cloths directly over his penis-head, which made it appear to be modeling some hot pink bonnet. I almost couldn't contain my amusement. Finally I got myself under control.

"Here, let me try," I said. We stopped in the middle of a soft sandy patch in the ground so I could take my shot at reconfiguring our one garment. I was just as unsuccessful. I removed the hat and attempted to fashion a coat instead, but it ended up behaving more like a loose scarf. Then I tried wrapping his penis up in the straps, so that it became like a highly ornamented barber shop pole. They wouldn't hold, and even worse, he had become erect from all the fiddling, so for the brief moment they did stay in place, it was a very poorly disguised cock indeed inside those spandex ribbons. After that I gave up, unwrapped him, and handed him back the top, which he promptly tossed over his head and at the foot of a large extra-bushy hedge beyond.

"Hey!" I said.

"You ever going to wear that again with the bottom missing?"

"Probably not," I admitted.

"You don't seem to be missing it much right now," he commented.

He was right. Ever since that hard cock had come out of its pink sleeve I'd been fondling it and was, even now, nearly humping his leg in an effort to wiggle it into my vagina. We were standing facing each other, and with the height differential we would have had to have been gods to make that work, but my body seemed unwilling to concede defeat as yet.

"That's a really big bush," Jesse whispered.

I looked at him quizzically. Was I supposed to be offended or flattered by that remark?

"No, there!" he said, reading my face and then tilting his head back over his shoulder. "That bush is big."

It was big, big enough to conceal two naked adults if someone approached it from the other side. We looked at each other with that unspoken mutual agreement again, and then he pushed me gently down to the ground and silently climbed on top of me. I buried my face in his chest and breathed deeply. God, he smelled good. My legs instinctively spread to admit him. The ground gave little, and I kept my hips down firm against it while he pushed up and into me from his own flattened position, breathing heavily but quietly.

It had only been a moment when we heard them, a multitude of increasingly audible voices that indicated that a crowd of people was drawing near. Jesse didn't pull out, but merely paused, bringing his face up to mine in a silent query. I shook my head and he jumped right back into it.

What a great friend, I thought. I took his shoulder between my teeth and used it to muffle my own heavy breathing while I fucked him back and waited apprehensively to see if they would chance upon us. The voices got louder, and finally became so clear that I could understand what they were saying. "Yes, that was a hell of a barbecue," and "I can't believe they invited everyone in the place," and although I was gratified to know why the lake had been so quiet up until now I really, really didn't want "everyone in the place" to interrupt the lovely private moment I'd been having with Jesse.

We kept it up for several more minutes, while the whole cavalcade passed right on the other side of the shrubbery, not ten feet from us. Jesse held it steady until all we could discern was the distant noise of twigs cracking, and then began pumping me hard and fast, as if he really meant it. I sensed that powerful stiffening inside that meant he was about to come and I panicked. Where was I going to clean up? I opened my mouth to tell him to pull out, but he was already out and leaning over me, holding his cock in his hand, jerking out every last bit of jizz and spilling it all over my tits until my nipples were white with the stuff. We lay there quietly for a while, panting, and that smell that had come from deep inside him rose up in waves all around me. It was more than I could take. I held my breath and concentrated instead on the feel of his juice drying on my skin until it almost felt like a garment, and I thought it funny that even without the top, my breasts hadn't ended up naked after all.

We made it the rest of the way back to the cabin without incident, and between meals managed to make love thrice more before it was time to go home. Each time Jesse came all over my chest and by the time we left the next day, my skin was so tacky I had trouble slipping into my shirt. I didn't shower for two days afterwards, and at least once an hour when I was alone I would stroke my fingers across my sticky breasts and think of him.

But the real trouble was, I guess I got used to having his smell all over me. Because when I finally gave in and washed myself off, I didn't feel right somehow. I smelled clean. I wanted to smell dirty again.

I think about that now as I lie next to Jesse, gently fondling his morning-stiffened cock and waiting for him to rouse into wakefulness. I've got an idea that maybe we should go back to the lake before the summer's over, after all. Some fresh air and clean water might do me some good. Because I hardly even need to suck his cock anymore to get a whiff of his juice. I can taste it in the air. My whole apartment smells like him now; I can't get rid of it. And I don't seem to be able to get rid of him, either.

"Morning," he says, pulling me close with a smile.

"Good morning, Jesse," I whisper back.

I bury my face in his chest. And I breathe.

"Weekend Away" is a modified excerpt from my first novel, *My Life with Michael: A Novel of Sex,*

Beer, and Middle Age. Publishing excerpts from your books is supposed to be a good method of raising interest in your work, and perhaps it is, but believe me, trying to turn a section of novel into a self-contained story is a heck of a lot more difficult than just writing a new story!

This is a perfect example. I thought I might like to use this segment, but it literally took me months to figure out what, outside of the context of my novel, the story was going to be about. The plot of my book simply wouldn't have made sense here, and I didn't want to play up the erotic elements too much because the sex was supposed to be secondary to the humor and the development of the relationship itself. I finally hit on the theme of Jesse's smell – which I thought nicely tied together the sexual and romantic aspects of the relationship – and by the time I finished working that in, I'll be darned if I hadn't become interested in what was going to happen to this new couple after the story ended. Who knows – maybe one day, they'll have a book to themselves!

LORI SCHAFER:
I WRITE EROTICA

In March of 2014, Guy Hogan, publisher of *The Pittsburgh Flash Fiction Gazette*, asked if he could feature me in a week-long special of pieces I had published on his site, along with an interview. Well, naturally I said, "Heck, yeah!" Well, that's what I said. What I wrote in response was more like "Dear Mr. Hogan, Thank you for this wonderful opportunity. I am truly honored that you wish to feature me…"

However, when I saw the interview questions, I wished that I had dispensed with the formalities, because these questions were anything but formal:

"Why do women suck cock and swallow cum?"

"Advice on eating pussy?"

56

Huh, I thought. I don't know how to answer those kinds of questions. And besides, since when am I a sexpert?

Well, I may not be a sexpert, but I can be a bit of a smartass, so this is how I responded:

Q. Why do women suck cock and swallow cum?

A. Smoking is bad for you. So are corn dogs. Cock is the healthy alternative when you want something long, warm, and tasty in your mouth.

Most women prefer to swallow cum when they can. It cuts down on both the laundry and the mopping.

Q. Advice on eating pussy?

A. Try it with a side of ice cream.

For some reason, Guy decided to make my questions harder.

Here's the full final interview:

Q: Lori, tell us a little about yourself.

A: Like most authors, I first became interested in writing as a child. I published my first piece of flash fiction in a local newspaper fifteen years ago - and then I stopped writing. I simply lost the creative impulse. I don't know where it went or why, but it was gone. I went to work in accounting, with which

I was quite happy for a time. Then about two years ago, I inexplicably got the urge to write again. I finished my first book – *My Life with Michael: A Story of Sex and Beer for the Middle-Aged* – in four months. Once I realized that no publisher was going to even look at my novel until I had some other credits to my name, I started writing short work – flash fiction, essays, memoirs – any idea I had, I wrote something about it. Within a year I had twenty-five publishing credits and finally felt confident enough to start sending my book around to publishers again. In the meantime, I completed my second novel, *Just the Three of Us*, an erotic romantic comedy that I dearly love – even after all the rewrites, it still cracks me up. I'm currently 120,000 words into a mega-monster of a novel entitled *On an Island: How One Woman Spent Twenty Years Shipwrecked On an Island with Sixteen Sailors and Lived to Tell the Tale*. I'm very enthusiastic about this book, but it's going to be so huge that I'm guessing it'll be at least a year before I finish it. Also, since I enjoyed *Just the Three of Us* so much, I've begun work on a sequel. Phew! Writing is exhausting.

Q: Why do you write erotica?

A: Sex is one of many subjects that I find intriguing. The sexual scenario is rife with possibilities for storytelling, and may be approached from countless different angles (no pun intended), from the dead serious to the outrageously comic. Personally, I tend to be most interested in stories about sex that aren't mainly for the purposes of titillation. To me, sex is an integral part of human life, and it's therefore only natural for it to be the central focus of many of our stories.

Q: What are peoples' reactions when they find out you write erotica?

A: If they know me at all, they're not very surprised.

Q: The media has reported that around 30% of American women consume porn on a regular basis. What do you think about that?

A: It doesn't surprise me a bit. Women have probably been consumers of pornographic materials for as long as men have; but in previous eras, the types of pornography that wcrc availablc to thcm were severely limited. Modern pornography is just the more sexually explicit version of the old-time "romances," and it certainly doesn't hurt that nowadays you can access all of the porn you want without having to go down to the adult book or video store and browse with all of the men. The internet has definitely decreased the embarrassment factor of consuming porn for both women and men, particularly, I think, for those who have kinky or fetishistic preferences. In addition, with more women now being involved in the production of pornography, it stands to reason that modern-day erotica is geared more towards women's tastes.

Q: Do you watch porn and if you do what is your favorite kind of porn to watch?

A: Of course. Except I call it "research."

I'm a woman of many moods - I don't have a particular favorite kind of porn.

Q: What advice do you have for women who want to write erotica?

A: Don't forget that the writing comes first, the sex second. If all you're writing about is he did this and she did that and it was hot, then your novel or story is not going to be as compelling as it could be. It's great to have a hot concept. But wording matters. Story structure matters. Writing sexy isn't enough. Be a writer first – the erotica will follow.

THE HANNELACK FANNY, OR HOW I LEARNED TO STOP WORRYING AND LOVE MY RUMP

"These don't fit either!" I exclaimed, utterly exasperated. I'd thought that buying clothes would be easier once I was a teenager, but instead it was turning into a nightmare any horror movie maker would have been proud to call his own.

My mother sighed, her tall, slender form dwarfed by the enormous pile of pants of every shape and style I had discarded and stacked by her side. She beckoned me to sit down beside her on the narrow dressing-room bench, but I was wedged too tightly into the last cantankerous pair of jeans to obey. I stood, futilely attempting to wriggle my way out of my denim prison while she looked me over, her eyes downcast and disconsolate.

"It's time for me to explain something to you, Janet," she said. "It's about your inheritance."

"My inheritance?" I said, surprised. Did she maybe have a secret supply of school clothes stashed away for me somewhere? I hoped so. I was so sick of all this fruitless shopping that I was nearly prepared to attend my new high school in our fancy Thanksgiving tablecloth, fringe and all.

She nodded. "Yes, dear. I'm afraid you've inherited… a family trait."

I glanced over at her and wondered what she could possibly be talking about; she and I didn't look a bit alike.

"It's called the Hannelack fanny," she blurted out. "All of the women on your father's side had it."

I giggled. Mom said "fanny."

"I'm glad you think it's funny," she said darkly. "But that's the reason why your rear-end won't fit into any of these jeans."

I gaped at her and fought the natural desire to look behind me at the object of this unexpected assault. Was she talking about my butt? And why did she look so serious all of a sudden?

"I'm sorry, sweetheart," she went on, shaking her head as glumly as if she'd just informed me that my new puppy had been diagnosed with an incurable form of doggy-cancer. "There's nothing we can do."

I felt my cheeks coloring – both sets. Suddenly I realized that I was standing with my back to the mirror. Even as we spoke, security guards might be staring at it, my big fat inheritance – the Hannelack fanny!

I dropped to the floor and felt the thick flesh fanning out beneath me like my own private carry-cushion. My mother stared curiously at me as she gathered up the pile of rejects. Naturally, as a normal-bottomed person, she wouldn't understand.

"I'll go pick out some skirts for you," she said, edging her way through the dressing-room door and closing it quietly behind her.

How I finally managed to wriggle my way out of those jeans, I can't recall. In fact, for weeks, even months afterward, my thoughts were so trained on the load I was hauling around in my caboose that for a time I forgot everything else. Before this little chat, I had hardly even noticed my bottom, tucked away out of sight and out of mind. Now I was constantly conscious of what lay barely concealed inside the granny panties I had, for some heretofore unknown reason, always insisted on wearing. I could feel it lurking there behind me, haunting my every footstep, like some soft-shoed prowler who had successfully slipped his big hands into my even bigger pockets. Never again would I forget it.

All at once, it was as if the cause of all of the most embarrassing moments of my young life came sharply into focus. It made so much sense now, I thought as I swiveled in front of my bedroom mirror, goggling over each enormous cheek in turn and trying to imagine what the pair looked like rear-on. That time I'd gotten stuck in the kiddie swing when I was five and the maintenance man had to come and cut me out. That memorable morning in the fourth grade when I'd ripped the seat of my pants making the winning walk under the limbo stick. And then there was that boy who'd spent most of last autumn chasing me down the street when I rode by him on my bike, snatching at my bottoms as I passed in an attempt to pull them down.

"I saw your a-ass! I saw your a-ass!" he'd sing out as my sweat-shorts came loose and dead leaves began collecting in my crack.

At the time it had seemed like an impressive achievement. Now it just sounded dumb. Evidently, I had a lot of ass to see.

It amazed me, how many years I'd gone without being aware of just how much junk I had packed in my trunk. This was why I'd never been able to perform a cartwheel. Why my elementary-school dresses were always too long in front and too short in back. Why I was the only kid in town who still used a banana bicycle seat. All my life, I'd been making molehills out of mountains, when all along I was sporting a topographical map of the Andes in my pants. It had to stop.

But an ass is not like a blemish that you can cover with a little makeup. It's not a bad haircut that grows out in a few weeks, or an ingrown toenail that eventually rights itself. It's your seat, your center, and it occupies a solid ten percent (or in my case, twenty) of your physical being. It's one of the two faces you show to the world – and it's the one that people stare at more often because they know you're not looking.

So I did what any other rational young woman with my special dilemma would do. Like poor Rudolph with his shiny red nose, I tried to hide my glaring white ass. Oh, I wouldn't say that the flouncy purple satin dress I wore to my prom was particularly successful. Nor were the black shorts I donned for gym class as slimming as the experts would have you believe, if the wide-angle photos that were taken of me playing volleyball can be deemed conclusive evidence. But by the time I reached college, not only had I learned how best to conceal my other half, I had also become rather adept at keeping it out of the public eye. I took the bus because the subway was too crowded; too many opportunities for presenting my posterior to those who were seated around me when I was forced to stand. I never climbed a flight of stairs if there was someone behind me, so that no poor unknowing creature could be confronted full in the face with the flesh of my fanny. I trained myself to sidle into rooms with my body tilted sideways, keeping my wall of a backside to the side facing the wall. I never got up to use the bathroom in the middle of class or, later, in the middle of a meeting at work. When I was at home I wore sweatpants and a T-shirt that fell to my thighs. But I never left the house in anything but a skirt or a dress, and control-top pantyhose with extra seams in the rear. I stopped wearing bright colors because I worried about looking like I had a circus tent draped over my own private big top. In the winter I wore a long, thick woolen coat; in summer, an oversized backpack that sat like an awning over a massive department store entrance.

It took a lot of focus and effort, covering up this bulging deformity. And as you might imagine, my deep self-consciousness over being cursed with this particular genetic defect put quite a strain on my love life. Oh, I had my share of boyfriends, but they never lasted very long. I was always happy to get naked with a fellow – just not with the lights on. And most men, it seemed, had some rather ludicrous expectations when it came to their sex lives.

"Oh, no, no," I'd say hastily if he tried to roll me over on top of him. "I really prefer to be on the bottom."

"Couldn't we change it up – just this once?"

Yeah, right. What if he tried to grab my ass? The rebound alone would send him flying.

"Oh, no, I don't think I want —"

"How about doggy-style, then?"

"Good God, no!"

You can imagine my horror at the thought of it. I envisioned my ass, pale from being so long relegated to darkness, hovering in the air surrounding us like some extra-white mushroom cloud, a certain sign that a disaster had just struck the surrounding area. Doggy-style, indeed!

But then, at last, along came John. John was special. John never tried to get me to "mix it up." He never asked me either to bend over or to get on top. He never wanted me to strip for him, and he never complained that I switched off the light before coming to bed. He respected the privacy of my lower half. He never even tried to wedge his face between my reluctant thighs, as some men did — as if I could risk allowing a man's eyes to come that close to the abundant and all-too-visible source of my deepest shame. In fact, he seemed perfectly content to hump me missionary-style over and over and over again — just as content as I was to let him.

Perhaps this was why, after we had been together for about a year, one night I let my guard down. It was but a minor lapse in my heretofore constant vigilance, but a nearly disastrous one.

I woke up around four a.m. one warm summer

night needing to use the toilet. John was snoring peacefully. We'd fallen asleep right after making love and we were both naked. Ordinarily if I got out of bed when he was over, I would slip on a robe to cover up my you-know-what, and then slip backwards out of bed to the bathroom. But this particular night was unusually hot and stuffy, and when I felt about on the floor and failed to find my robe in its usual spot, I decided to take a chance.

It wasn't really much of a gamble. In all the nights we had spent together, I had never once known John to be awakened before daylight, not even the night Mr. Withers from down the hall lost his parrot and came banging on the apartment door at one a.m. to see if we had stolen it.

There was no break in John's snoring as I slipped silently out of bed. I went and did my business, then returned to the bedroom. By a glint of moonlight shining in through the open window, I spotted my robe on the floor by the base of the bed. I bent to pick it up.

All of a sudden the lights kicked on and I froze. Quickly I placed my hands over my ass. It was like trying to cover a pothole with a pebble.

I shrieked and jumped back into bed with my legs spread, hoping that the sight of my more appealing nether region would serve as a distraction. It didn't.

"What the hell was that?!" John cried. The long-dreaded words were still echoing in my ears when I felt him grabbing for my hindquarters. I scooted to the far edge of the bed, planting all of my weight on my butt, where it spread out beneath me, as smooth as creamy peanut butter on a warm English muffin.

He lunged; reached out with his huge hands and grasped me hard about the hips. With one fluid motion, he flipped me over, exposing my giant naked ass for all the world to see.

I heard a sharp intake of breath. It was over, I thought miserably as I struggled to wiggle free and felt my flesh rippling in waves behind me. How many years had I been expecting this, this cruel revelation of my most shocking feature, and butt-naked, no less. I tried to roll over to bury my offending bottom, but he had me pinned tight to the mattress. There was nothing for it but to lie still and minimize the jiggling while I dreaded the inevitable double-talk and the quick exit that were sure to come next.

Still he was silent. I felt a warm breeze drifting in through the open window, tickling the tiny soft hairs that covered my chubby soft cheeks. It made my ass feel light and unconstrained, as if it had never been let out into the open before. I pondered how long it had been, since my rump had, indeed, felt the sweet touch of fresh air. Then I thought of my neighbors across the courtyard and wondered if they could see it, or if it was visible to one of the many satellites circling the earth and I would see it myself on the ten o'clock news, accompanied by a news anchor's crack about gravitational pull.

And then I heard a heavy sigh and remembered my companion, and that this was the moment in which it was ending between us.

"Why didn't you tell me about this?' he whispered, the expulsion of his breath striking between my cheeks like some very soft paddle. I shifted uncomfortably but he was still holding me down and I didn't dare to speak.

"Why didn't you tell me about this?" he said again.

I waited, expecting him to back away. He removed his hands from my hips and I felt them growing cool in his absence. But then I felt warm fingertips returning to my thighs, climbing, even, up along them, towards the forbidden hills that overlooked them.

"John," I began, meaning to tell him to stop.

"Hush," he replied. I heard the bedsprings squeak. He was shifting position.

And for the first time in my life, I felt, like silky spiders creeping up beyond my legs, the glorious touch of hands on my ass.

Oh, it was ecstasy, the purest, sweetest ecstasy, those fingers tickling across my bum! How gently he stroked it, how delicately he ran his thumbs over the soft skin, which quivered excitedly in response!

And then he took those big hands and spread them, like rainbows, across my cheeks, so that I felt the warmth of his fingertips falling upon my backside like brilliant rays of midsummer sun. And before I had even adjusted myself to this wonderful new sensation, before I had even considered the possibility that my ass could give me pleasure as well as pain, he squeezed.

All at once shock waves rippled throughout my whole body, and I cried out, tensing my buttocks into his grip as I did so, and feeling him grip me harder in return, pressing his fingers into the fat of my ass as if it were dough he was kneading in preparation of the most delicious treat you could ever imagine.

I heard joyous laughter. Most of it was coming from me. Then I felt a chest descending down over my backside, and a breath riffling my ear.

"You like that, don't you?" John said, giving my ass another ecstasy-inducing squeeze.

"Eeeeee!" I squealed.

He laughed again. "If only you'd showed me sooner," he said, "I would have brought some assistants. An ass this glorious needs eight hands to do it justice!"

He repositioned his fingers and clutched me again. The tension went straight to my loins and I shuddered, wondering how my single neighbor would feel about being appointed an assistant.

"But we will have to make do." He withdrew, and once again my cheeks knew the fresh feel of clean air whispering across them. The bed creaked and I glanced over my shoulder. He was getting into a kneeling position. He was bending forward. He was pursing his lips. No, I thought. He isn't! No one would want to… he isn't!

He planted a firm wet kiss right in the center of my left cheek, then another right beneath it. Another, then another, trickling a trail of wetness across the vast field of flesh, little spots of saliva that tickled my skin as they cooled and dried. I wriggled and squirmed in my excitement. Then he took hold of me again with his two firm hands and moved his mouth over to my right cheek, kissing it all over in turn, and then returning, very slowly, very gradually, back to the center. I held my breath and waited.

"You like that?" he said again.

"Yes, please," I whispered.

"How about that?" he whispered, planting his lips very daintily along the top of my crack.

I gulped. "Yes, please," I said again.

I felt his hands move and my butt move with them. I felt the skin lifting and separating, the two halves of my bottom parting company like massive double-doors which have just been cranked open to let in the sun. He was spreading my cheeks apart.

I gasped as I felt his lips landing further down

my crack. I gasped again as he touched his tongue even lower. Then with a great heave, he shoved the rest of my ass-fat aside, exposing my deepest, darkest hole.

"Yes, please," I repeated automatically.

He didn't answer. But the next moment I felt something warm and wet snaking its way into my crack.

"Oh, dear God!" I yelled as hands yanked me up onto all fours, throwing my giant rump up into the stratosphere like a shiny new statue, where it stood proudly on display for any and all who cared to pay the two bits to see it. And for once I didn't care; I was glad, glad to be showing my ass, glad to be exhibiting it in all its wondrous glory. And while I was reveling in my newfound ass-freedom, he grabbed hold of my cheeks as if they were handles and then lifted them, lifted them so that his cock could slither its way beneath the fat and into my pussy. He shoved and I moaned, feeling for the first time his balls slapping my rear, understanding, for the first time, how much fun I'd been missing. He shoved again, harder, and they slapped me harder, thwack, thwack, as they bounced delightfully against my newfound joy, my treasure, my big, bare ass!

Naturally that was only the beginning. Once my secret was exposed, John made no bones about making my big bottom the big center of his attention.

"Why hello there!" he'd exclaim, pushing his way boldly past me into my apartment and getting behind me with clasping hands outstretched. "What have you got for me today?"

"Not much," I'd giggle, bouncing on my toes and setting my whole rump to rippling.

"Not much?" he'd disagree, shaking his head. "From where I stand, you've got a lot. Two giant fistfuls, in fact!"

He'd throw me down on the bed with my butt in the air and I'd clap with delight while he grabbed it and squeezed it and kissed it and licked it and then he'd take me, his hands and balls slapping me softly from behind. Suddenly I couldn't get enough of getting fucked from behind.

It didn't stop in the bedroom, though. Oh, no. I'd finally learned to accept the ass I'd been dealt, to relish and enjoy it. How much pleasure I had denied myself, all these years of trying to tame it! How long I had kept it hiding when I should have been flaunting it, showing it off, making sure it got the treatment it so sorely deserved!

I had to make up for lost time. I owed it to my ass.

I gave away all of my clothes, all of the frumpy dresses and long skirts beneath which I'd been concealing my greatest asset. I tossed all of my pantyhose, their seams stretched to their limits. I even got rid of the granny-briefs and replaced them with sexier underwear.

John's eyes goggled as I lifted the back of my skirt to show him.

"Is that a thong?" he said, his eyes shining delightedly.

"No, bikini," I said. Confused, I turned to look behind me. The backside of my panties had vanished into the valley of my crack.

"Close enough!" he answered, rubbing his hands all over my bared ass-skin.

I bought dresses that flared about me when I twirled, and miniskirts that clung like plastic wrap to my thighs. I gave up crotchless stockings and made them buttless instead. I loved that because if I walked quickly or bent over, I could feel the breeze on my ass. How I loved the feel of the breeze on my ass!

I even finally started running, down at the park in the center of town. Not, sad to say, because I wanted the exercise. Oh, no. I wanted to wear short-shorts that let my buttocks hang out the bottom as I jogged. It made me giggle to feel them bouncing as I ran. I giggled even harder when jaws dropped as I passed.

One weekend a few months later, John and I went on a road trip. I'd leaned over sideways and lifted my skirt up over my hips so that he could rest his hand on my ass while he was driving. Sunshine was streaming through the open sunroof and my butt felt warm in spite of its near-nakedness. How I relished that sensation now!

Suddenly a truck horn sounded.

"Hey!" I heard a man yell. "Hey, wide load!"

A year before, I would have been mortified. Not anymore.

I turned to look. A semi was travelling beside us. The man in the passenger seat was staring at my bared ass. The driver was leaning over, trying to get a look.

"Like what you see, boys?" I yelled back, jerking my body in my seat to set my rump to rippling.

"WOOOO-EEEE! Shake that ass, mama!"

In that moment, something possessed me. It was as if the beast that had so long been bolted to my bottom had finally broken free of its cage. It wanted out. All the way out.

I unhooked my seatbelt and jumped up on my seat. With effort I wriggled my way through the open sunroof, ass and all. And then I wiggled out of my panties, lifted up my skirt, and showed myself to the world. Every last wobbling inch of me.

"Look at my ass!" I yelled, slapping it hard with my palm. "Look at my ass!"

I was bouncing, jumping up and down in place, and my ass, behemoth that it was, was bouncing, too, the fat landing on the warm roof of the car and then retreating back up to my waist in happy rhythm while I pointed and laughed.

"Look at my ass!"

There was no need to yell; everyone was already looking. All around us, it seemed, cars were honking and people were staring and another truck had pulled up alongside us and was blaring its big horn in rhythm to my dance.

"Look at my ass!" I shouted gleefully again, turning around backwards so I could shake my butt at the cars in front.

That was when I saw that a police car had overtaken us. I felt a hand tugging at my ankle and knew that John had seen it, too.

"Come down!" he hissed.

I tried. I really did try. But I simply couldn't get my butt to cooperate. Now that it was up, it refused to go back down.

It was too late, anyway. The cruiser's lights were already flashing and John was pulling over; I could hear him cursing beneath me. Stroking my rear for luck, I waited patiently while he parked and the cop pulled up behind him. People were still honking. I shook my big butt and waved cheerfully back at them.

I heard a burst of static and the tinny sound of a faraway voice. A lady-cop was standing next to the car, a radio clipped to her waist.

"Good afternoon, officer," John stuttered.

"Sir," she answered vaguely. Her eyes were trained on me.

"Excuse me, Miss," she called. "Mind telling me what you're doing up there?"

My ass was still warm from the sunshine and exercise. And people were still honking.

Unh-unh, I thought. I'm not chaining it up again. My fanny had fought hard for its freedom; it had earned the right to savor the spoils!

"Showing off my giant ass," I answered blithely.

I saw her giving me the once-over. She didn't seem impressed.

"Would you come down from there, please?" she said.

"I can't," I admitted. "My butt won't fit back through the hole."

For a second I thought a flicker of sympathy shone in her eyes. Then she said, "Climb over the roof then," and she watched me as I hauled my ass up awkwardly over the ledge and down the side of the car.

I rearranged my skirt over my thighs and took my place by the driver's side door. I glanced at John. He did not look pleased.

"I don't know what came over her, Officer," he said in a rush. "Normally she keeps her big butt to herself. I never would have let her do it if I had known that's what she was planning."

Something about the way he said that really rubbed me the wrong way. Was he criticizing me for displaying my ass? My ass and I didn't think we liked that very much. Besides, since when was he in charge of what me and my ass did?

"Uh-huh," the policewoman answered. She reached into her jacket and pulled out a pad. This is it, I thought, I'm going to jail. My ravishing rump would be ruined by rough prison toilets and wasted away by poor prison foods. Well, I thought, patting it absentmindedly, at least we had a good run. Short, but good.

She handed me a slip of paper. It had a lot of fine print and some impressive dollar signs on it.

"Riding without a seatbelt is dangerous," she said, shaking a finger at me. "Don't do it again."

She turned and walked away. I gaped after her, speechless. And saw, wedged onto the back of her skinny frame, an ass the size of which put my bony little bottom to shame.

I looked back at John. He was gaping, too.

"Never mind that now!" he snapped. "Get in!"

That incident marked a turning point for John and me. He wasn't the type to argue or yell, but I could tell that he was mad. For the first time in months, he didn't touch my ass. Not that night or the next, nor the week or the month after that.

"Come on, John!" I'd whine, backing my posterior into him with all of the subtlety of a four-alarm fire. "Just touch it, will ya?"

"Forget it!" he'd snort, determinedly training his eyes on the wall behind my behind. He refused to relent. No touches, no tickles, no kisses, no licks. It was as if he'd decided that he had unleashed a monster, and was doing his best to stuff it back in its cage.

But of course he couldn't. No, you can't undo something like that once it's been done. And it was no surprise to me that we didn't last too long after that, John and I. He said I'd gotten a little too wild for him, and maybe he was right. He had certainly gotten too tame for me.

We didn't lack for company or entertainment long, though. My ass and I aren't so shy anymore. In fact, you might say we're downright sociable, as my new boyfriend Robert would certainly agree.

I met him in the library just two weeks after John and I split up. I was wiggling my way down the aisle past the study tables when I heard a heavy book drop. I looked over my shoulder and saw an attractive young man sitting behind a stack of tomes, staring at me with his mouth agape.

"Hello!" I said cheerfully, giving my rump a shake so that it waved at him.

"Pardon me, Miss," he said, tearing his eyes, with an effort, away from my jiggling rear. "It's just such a coincidence that you happened to pass by as I was reviewing the latest research on women with your condition."

"My condition?"

"The size of your posterior," he explained,

unabashed. "It's quite glorious, you know."

I felt my cheeks turning pink. They'd never received a compliment quite like that before.

"Um, thank you," I said, thinking I could take a liking to this frank and direct young scholar who was pursuing such a fascinating subject of study. "And what exactly are the results of this research?"

"Well, for one thing, it's been scientifically proven that large buttocks make for a more highly pleasurable sexual experience," he said, dropping his glasses to the edge of his nose and giving my curves the once-over a second and third time around.

"Really?!" I squealed. Not that I would have argued the point – I knew better than anyone how right he was.

"Little, Little, Stickman et al," he said with authority, digging around in his bag and finally emerging with a slide rule. "Would you mind?" he said, gesturing to me to turn around.

I turned and he knelt down behind me. My rump seemed to sense him back there; it was growing warm and tingly. I felt the ruler slapping gently against my cheeks, sending shock waves shivering throughout my body. It had been some time since anyone but me had touched my ass. I'd nearly forgotten how amazing it felt.

"As I suspected," he nodded to himself, evidently ignorant of the effect he was having on my overly sensitive backside. "According to their research, your buttocks are quite nearly perfect. They fit the prescribed ratios to within ninety-six percent."

I gazed down at him in awe. My Hannelack fanny? Perfect?

"I must confess, Miss," he continued, blushing, "I am rather partial to a woman with a solid seat. I don't suppose I might persuade you to join me in a cup of coffee?"

The three of us have been inseparable ever since.

There's no question that Robert truly is special to both me and my ass. Not even John ever developed such an intimate relationship with my better half. The pleasure in my posterior goes deeper for Robert, I suspect. Where John admired, he adores. Where John caressed, he cradles. Where John licked, he deep-kisses. Where John squeezed, he spanks. Oh, yes – he spanks.

"Bend over, sweetheart," he says with a smile, flexing his fingers in preparation. "Let's see what you've got."

I give him what I've got. And then some.

How I shiver and shake when I feel the flats of his palms striking my flesh, punishing and yet praising, every blow a joy to him to deliver and to me to receive! How filled I am with contentment when he's rubbing me down afterwards, spreading lotion in lazy circles over my blazing red cheeks, pausing every so often to give them a long, wet, dazzling kiss!

"Help me hold your cheeks open," he says at last, and I reach back and hold them, knowing that no two hands alone could possibly handle them both. I turn and look over my shoulder and I gasp in delight as I see his face vanish, feel his sweet lips on my asshole, his tongue poking and prodding, exploring my anus. How at peace I feel when he emerges many minutes later, his face shining, his mouth tired but so very pleased, so very delighted! Never could I have dreamed of a man who would treat my rump with such astonishing respect and devotion. Never could I have dreamed of a man who would so utterly dedicate himself to bringing it pleasure.

It's because of Robert that I thank heaven I'm a Hannelack. Otherwise I might never have gotten this fanny.

And in the evenings when we're lying naked together, his arms clasped firmly around my oh-so-chubby cheeks, the conviction grows within me that the time has finally arrived. To share with him the grandest privilege, the supreme honor. To at last delve with him into this, my darkest, most mysterious cavern; to uncover the treasures buried deepest inside me. To finally give to my ass the greatest gift I can give it, the ultimate expression of love and affection.

I picture it often. I'll turn and lift my skirt and give my rump a shake that will vibrate the windows and rattle the doors. Then I'll drop down to my knees and bend over before him, so bold, so brazen, just like my ass. I'll grip my cheeks with my hands and spread them apart, feel my ass opening up, inviting him in, feel it glowing with the knowledge that it no longer has to be sad, no longer has to be lonely. It will tingle with excitement, with anticipation and happiness, with heartfelt yearning for a pleasure that I've too long denied it. For a pleasure I will never again need to deny it.

"Robert?" I'll say sweetly, gazing back at him over my shoulder with reverence and trust in my eyes. "Would you please make love to my ass?"

And he will. He'll pull aside my buttocks and smile, knowing what joy we are about to give him, knowing what joy he is about to give us. With prodding tongue and probing fingers he'll gradually work his way in, patiently waiting for my asshole to accept those small bits of his body before he pushes it further. Then when the moment is right, and my ass and I are relaxed and ready for more, he'll apply lubrication, oiling us up until we're as slippery and inviting as a cool waterslide on a midsummer's day. Then, oh, so slowly, so sweetly, so gently, inch by lovely, delicate inch, he'll penetrate into it, into me, into us, into the very essence of my innermost being, through the asshole that has become such an integral part of my soul. He'll slowly slide his way in and then slide his way out, over and over while I tremble and moan, sprawled beneath him in a position that's so vulnerable and yet, with him, so utterly safe. I'll focus on the feel of him touching my insides, stroking me deep underneath; I'll take his sweet, gentle back-and-forth rhythm until sweet is no longer enough, until gentle will no longer do.

Then I'll cry out, in my ecstasy and want, "Please, Robert, please! Pound me! Give my ass the pounding it so sorely deserves!"

And he'll do that, too. He'll press into me, the last two inches that he's been reserving, until I feel the hairs on his balls tickling my cheeks. And then he'll hold himself there, deep, deep inside me, and he'll spank my ass hard so that I feel the same tingle both inside and out. Then he'll wedge my cheeks open and throw himself between them, plunging and plunging until I'm screaming with pleasure, until I feel so incredible that I can no longer stand it. And just when I think that I can no longer stand it, he'll release his load, way, way down, deep in the heart of me, so deep that I'll be able to feel it, squirming warm and wet inside of my hole.

I'll lie there, spent, my ass in the air while he kisses every inch of my worn-out cheeks. I'll smile as he wraps his arms around my hips and hangs onto my rump like it's the most precious gem on the planet. And I'll wait. I'll wait until I feel Robert's pressure again increasing, his cock growing stiff where it rests, peacefully nuzzled between my soft, warm cheeks. I'll wait until the pressure has once again built inside of me, too, inside of my ass. And then I'll ask what I know I need to ask, what I know my ass wants me to ask.

"Can we do that again?"

He'll be happy to do it. For me, for us. Me and my Hannelack fanny. Glorious. Wild. And free.

How well I remember the day she broke it to me, my poor mother, the unfortunate soul who had to advise me of the curse of inheritance that had fallen upon me. How disturbed I was by it, particularly its unusual moniker. Other people had family traits that had been passed down from generation to generation. But you never heard anything about the "Smith ears" or the "Johnson nose." Why did the shape and size of my rear have to be so famous that it was christened after a whole family line? The Hannelack fanny, indeed!

Mom exaggerated, of course. My butt was not that big; merely, perhaps, a bit out of proportion to the rest of my body. Or rather, thanks to years of running and ice hockey, that's how it is now. I seem to recall a mound of far greater size constantly threatening to protrude from my jeans or my shorts or from underneath my skirts. I definitely recall the struggle to find bottoms that fit. And ripping my pants in that limbo contest. And that stupid boy who was always trying to yank down my shorts.

In this story I thought it would be funny to follow the imaginary journey of a woman who suffered from a similar – if considerably larger – predicament, to trace her response to her "deformity" from first knowledge to final glory. When I started writing it, I didn't have any idea where it would lead. But by the time I got to the end, it was obvious where it had to go – the only place it could go.

Personality-wise, I don't have much in common with the woman in the story – you'll never catch me shaking anything of mine in public! – but I can definitely empathize with her on one specific point. Perhaps the most disturbing part of having a sizeable posterior is that you can't ever really see what it looks like, not as other people see it, anyway. You can look at each half sideways, but that only gives you an obstructed view. You can get a pretty decent three-quarters view in the mirror, but then it's always tilted and your perspective is warped. I suppose if you really wanted to know, you could set up a camera on a timer and simply get into a relevant position or two. In fact, nowadays I guess you could pretty easily make a video and simply play it back for yourself on your phone. Just think, after all these years, I can finally see what it truly looks like – my big fat rump – the Hannelack fanny!

But you know, on second thought…

I don't think I want to know.

OTHER BOOKS BY THE AUTHOR

JUST THE THREE OF US

Three close friends get too close for comfort in *Just the Three of Us: An Erotic Romantic Comedy for the Commitment-Challenged.*

Meet Kathy, a thirty-seven-year-old drifter who's constantly on the move: to new towns, new jobs, and new relationships. Imagine her surprise when she's befriended by lifelong friends Sam and Ted, attractive young men who, though ten years her junior, are far more settled than she thinks she'll ever be. Cheer them on as their three-way friendship succumbs to passion, then passion to romance, and romance to… well, surely it couldn't be love. Could it?

With a well-earned Heat Level of 4+, dialogue guaranteed to make you laugh out loud, and a plot to tickle your most sentimental of spots, *Just the Three of Us* promises an entertaining read for fans of romance looking for a unique take on love and sexuality.

Now available in paperback (both standard and large print sizes) and in eBook at retailers worldwide.

Excerpt from *Just the Three of Us:*

Ted lay calmly beside me, his hand resting lightly on my hip, seeming perfectly at ease. His fingers took a few tentative steps down my thighs and warmth flooded into them. I guess it showed because he smiled meaningfully at me. I smiled back, my knees parting subtly in welcoming expectation.

I heard heavy breathing in my other ear. I turned to look and saw that Sam was hyperventilating.

"Are you all right?" I said, stroking my fingers against his chest.

"Are we going to…?" he choked, panting with the effort of speaking. "We are, aren't we?'

"We don't have to," I said uncertainly.

"We don't?"

I put on my bravest face and tried to swallow my eagerness. I felt Ted's fingers pressing into my thigh and disappointment overcame me again. I forced it down. We were friends first, after all. Even if I could pressure him into this, I wouldn't.

"Not if you don't want to," I assured him.

He swallowed and gazed thoughtfully into my eyes. Behind my back, Ted remained silent.

"But you want to, don't you?"

I shrugged away my ardor with effort. "It's not all about me," I said.

I saw him glance over my shoulder and knew he was looking at Ted.

"It's not that I don't want to," he mumbled. "I'm just… I'm just not sure I'm ready."

Ted laughed loudly behind my back, breaking the tension, and I swiveled towards him, startled.

"This is all you've talked about all week!" he roared, rolling his body forward into mine.

"What?!" I said, turning back to look at Sam. He was grinning rather sheepishly.

"Night and day," Ted confirmed, his hand abandoning my thigh and tightly circling my waist instead. "How he absolutely couldn't wait one more minute and couldn't we get you to come over sooner and did I think you'd really go through with it."

"Well, I…" Sam protested feebly, his cheeks coloring as he lapsed again into that sheepish grin.

"So the truth comes out!" I laughed.

"Hey, it's totally different now that you're actually here! I still can't believe…"

"Believe it, buddy!" I interrupted and he gaped at me, surprised by my sudden change in tone. "Now get your butt over here before I lose my temper. It's not polite to keep a woman waiting," I said severely.

"Yes, ma'am!" he said, sliding into me with all of the force and enthusiasm of mud on a California hillside. "Miss!" he hurriedly corrected himself.

"That's better!" I asserted. "Now by the time I count ten, I expect to be in bed with two very handsome and very naked young men. No more dilly-dallying!" I threatened, wagging my finger at them. "One…"

Abruptly they both jerked away from me, and I rolled onto my backside and watched as polo shirts and boxers went flying across the room like kites snapping in a spring breeze.

"Eight," I breathed, but they were already done. They rolled sideways against me where I still lay flat on my back and then snuggled up close to each side of me, their cheeks pink with excitement. I sensed the weight of their bodies pushing against me from my chest to my legs; felt the sweat forming where their skin was pressed against mine. And into each of my hips poked something hard but soft; deliciously promising and hopelessly decadent, and I gulped, uncertain whether to savor the sensation or run away from it.

Maybe I, too, had the tiniest of doubts about this.

MY LIFE WITH MICHAEL

My Life with Michael: A Novel of Sex, Beer and Middle Age is a romantic fantasy for anyone who has ever wanted to have their beer and drink it, too. Surprisingly sweet, the story follows the course of an adulterous affair between two ordinary people confronting the changes that aging brings to the experience of love and sexuality. With humor and honesty, my novel explores the pleasures and pitfalls of the adulterous relationship: the crudity of the courtship, the raw sexuality that ultimately lapses into monotony, and, inevitably, the bittersweet farewell.

Now available in paperback (both standard and large print sizes) and in eBook at online retailers worldwide.

Excerpt from *My Life with Michael*:

When I crept around the next corner, fingers clenched to the steering wheel as if it were a life preserver, the street sign told me it was the right one and there I was, driving into the hotel parking lot at last. I still had twenty minutes to spare. Why wasn't it over yet?!

I sat absolutely still for five of those minutes, mentally commanding my heart to cease its infernal yammering. I spent the next five gathering up my things and checking to make sure that all of the windows and doors were locked and the parking brake was set six or seven times. And then it was ten till and I still had to get to the tenth floor and I figured I'd better hurry because I didn't want to be late. What was this, a job interview?

Contempt for my own foolishness finally got me going. I made it through the lobby and all the way up the stairs to the tenth floor without hesitating, and then I was in his hallway and the room was right there, but I was panting and sweating and I couldn't go in just yet. Unless I was going up to the thirty-eighth floor or I had a lot of baggage or companions, I always took the stairs, and now I regretted that age-old resolve on my part because I was a mess and even worse, I'd lost my physical momentum and had started thinking again about what was going to happen here. Big mistake.

The hallway was high-ceilinged and dim. Phony candle-type lanterns hung in iron brackets every ten feet along the walls, spilling what little there was of their eerie light onto the blood-red carpet. The only windows to the outside were at the very ends of the protracted hallways; I could barely make out the tiny breaks they carved into the pervasive gloom. I wondered whether they were large enough for me to jump through. Hoping for respite from the strangling sensation that clutched at my throat, I craned my neck skyward. The ceiling was decorated with some sort of bronze gilded pattern, and where a moment before it had given the impression of loftiness, now it seemed to be pressing down, ever closer to my unprotected skull, and the gilding wasn't an artistic design, it was a web of interlocking chains poised to drop down and trap me there, where Michael would undoubtedly find me the next morning, huddled in a whimpering ball and ready for the insane asylum. I peeked reluctantly back towards his door. It stood tall and ominous, a large black iron knocker dead in its center. "Boom! Boom! Boom!" I seemed to hear it clamor, surely in order to summon the damned spirits within. "Boom! Boom! Boom!" And then there was a slow creaking sound, like that of a poorly oiled door or the gates of hell opening, and I leapt into the air and from that elevated vantage point finally saw that there was a visitor entering another room down at the other end of the hall.

I exhaled. Somewhere in my head I heard chicken noises and that was annoying so I ran a brush through my now mostly dry hair, resettled my bag on my shoulder, and took a fortifying deep breath that I wished was a beer. I took the teeniest hold possible of that big black knocker and gave it the most timid tap I could muster. "Boom!" it resounded. I heard movement inside the room, and then a chasm was opening before my eyes, threatening to swallow me up, and I held my breath as the door separated slowly from its jamb. I don't mind telling you that in that moment I was scared out of my wits and not in the least bit horny. And when he finally appeared in the doorway the expression on his face told me that he felt about the same way.

"Hi," I said. As usual I'd chosen the best moment to show off my quick wit and brilliant conversational skills.

"Hi," he answered back, with equally impressive eloquence.

And then we stared at each other, motionless with fear.

"Can I come in?" I asked finally, speculating with some justification that the answer might be no.

"Oh, of course." He moved aside about three inches, and I wiggled my way out of the hallway and into the room.

ABOUT THE AUTHOR

Lori Schafer is a writer of serious prose and humorous erotica and romance – because she thinks sex is as funny as it is fun. Her books explore nontraditional sexual and romantic relationships as well as the changes that occur in love with age. Her first two novels – *My Life with Michael: A Novel of Sex, Beer, and Middle Age*, and *Just the Three of Us: An Erotic Romantic Comedy for the Commitment-Challenged* – were released early in 2015. She is currently at work on a sequel to *Just the Three of Us* as well as an epic mega-monster of a novel entitled *On An Island: How One Woman Spent Twenty Years On An Island with Sixteen Sailors and Lived to Tell the Tale.* You can learn more about Lori and her forthcoming projects by visiting her website at lorilschafer.com or by subscribing to her erotic book newsletter at http://eepurl.com/bfDVcn.

"We Are All Miss America"

BOOK CLUB QUESTIONS

1. Which of these stories did you like best? Why?

2. What did you think of the author's use of her own personal experiences in writing some of these stories? Did you enjoy knowing the history?

3. What did you think of the author's use of humor? Was the style of writing not what you expected?

4. As the author points out, there's a certain discomfort in being a writer of erotica that doesn't come into play for someone who writes in other genres. How do you think you would feel if your boss or your parents or your high school algebra teacher read your erotic works? How would you respond to their inquiries?

5. Would you ever consider writing sexy stories yourself (or have you tried it already)? Who would you want to read your work?

6. What do you think would be a good premise for an erotic short story? Would it mainly be sexual, or also romantic? What kinds of characters would be involved? Where would the story take place?

www.ingramcontent.com/pod-product-compliance
Lightning Source LLC
Chambersburg PA
CBHW020324130626
46549CB00003B/1011